Material Matters
Glass

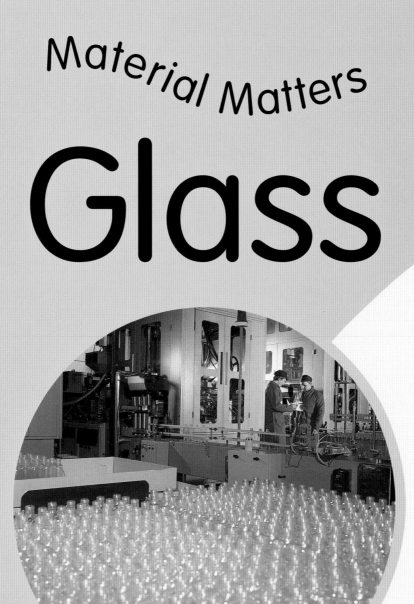

Terry Jennings

Chrysalis Children's Books

First published in the UK in 2003 by
Ⓒ Chrysalis Children's Books
An imprint of Chrysalis Books Group Plc
The Chrysalis Building, Bramley Road,
London W10 6SP

Text by Terry Jennings

ISBN 1-84138-821-1

British Library Cataloguing in Publication Data
for this book is available from the British Library.

Editorial Manager: Joyce Bentley
Series Editor: Sarah Nunn
Design: Stonecastle Graphics Ltd
Picture Researcher: Paul Turner

Printed in China

10 9 8 7 6 5 4 3

Picture credits:
Corbis: page 24 © James L. Amos/Corbis.
Firefly Glass/Dan Aston: pages 10-11.
Pilkington plc: pages 4, 8-9, 12-13, 19.
Roddy Paine Photographic Studios: pages 5 (below), 16, 17 (top and below right), 18 (below), 20, 21 (right), 22, 26, 28-29.
Spectrum Colour Library: pages 5 (top), 27.
Stonecastle Graphics: pages 6-7, 18 (top), 23 (below), 25 (top).
Sylvia Cordaiy Photo Library: pages 17 (below left), 23 (top).
United Glass Ltd: pages 14-15.

Contents

Using glass

Glass is one of our most important **materials**. Windows are made of glass so that we can see through them. Some buildings are made almost completely of glass.

Lots of buildings have walls made of glass.

One of the first large glass buildings was the Crystal Palace in London. It was finished in 1851 but burned down in 1936.

Light bulbs and light tubes are made from glass.

The lens of a camera is made from glass.

Drinking glasses and many jugs are made of glass. Glass used for cooking has to be very tough. Glass can also be beautiful. Many **ornaments** are made of glass.

Early glass

Nobody knows who first discovered how to make glass.

More than 5,000 years ago the ancient Egyptians were using glass jugs and vases. The Egyptians were also the first people to make coloured glass.

Natural glass – a piece of quartz rock crystal.

The Romans were the first people to use glass for windows.

Whoever discovered glass, may have lit a fire in a sandy place and later found little pieces of the hard, clear substance we call glass amongst the sand. The sand and ashes would have heated together to make glass.

Very old windows often have a thick patch in the middle. This is called a 'bull's eye'.

Making glass today

Today we still use sand to make glass. But instead of using ashes, we use two substances called soda and lime. The sand, soda and lime are heated in a large **furnace**. They **melt** and join together to make glass.

Sand, soda and lime being heated in a furnace to make glass.

Glass for windows has to be very flat. It is made by floating molten glass on a bath of molten tin.

The **molten** glass is a clear **liquid**, like water. When the glass cools, it hardens and forms a **solid** we can see through.

Glass blowing

Glass can be formed into different shapes by glass blowing. The glass-blower dips a long metal tube into molten glass and then blows down the tube into the molten glass.

The **glass-blower** dips a metal tube in hot, molten glass.

The glass gets bigger like a soap bubble. The glass-blower is able to change the shape of the bubble of glass before it cools. Liquid, or molten, glass can be made into many different shapes, including wine glasses, vases and paperweights.

This glass-blower blows down a long tube to make the molten glass grow bigger, like a balloon.

The finished decorative glass paperweight.

Window glass

Glass is used to make windows because we can see through it. We say glass is **transparent**. Window glass must have a smooth surface if we are to see through it clearly.

Glass for windows being melted in a furnace.

Window glass is made by floating molten glass on top of a bath of molten tin. The molten glass cools and hardens to form a smooth layer.

Window glass is cooled carefully so that it does not crack.

The largest windows in the world are in a building in Paris, France. They are 50 metres high and 218 metres wide.

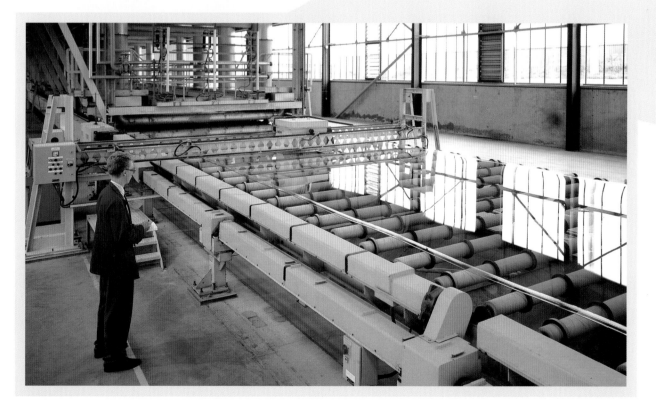

Glass jars

Glass jars, bottles and light bulbs are made by machines in a special factory. To make a jar, a blob of molten glass is dropped into a shape called a **mould**.

Most glass milk bottles are filled, used and then cleaned at least 30 times before they are melted down and made into new bottles.

This factory makes thousands of glass bottles every day.

A machine then blows air
into the blob of molten glass
to fill the shape of the mould.
The jar is put into a hot oven
to make it stronger. When the
jar is cool again, it is ready to use.

These new
bottles are
cooling down
before they
are filled
and labelled.

Glass for decoration

Many ornaments are made of glass. Glass is used because of its beauty, shape, colour and sparkle.

This glass was decorated using tiny drills and grinding wheels to make the patterns.

The surface of glass can be cut and decorated. Patterns can be made on the glass. Sometimes a jet of sand is fired at a glass object to make the surface look 'frosty'. Glass can also be coloured by mixing in coloured substances while it is still molten.

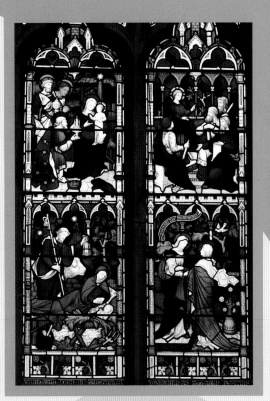

A stained glass window is made from hundreds of tiny pieces of coloured glass.

This glass animal had to be shaped while the glass was hot and molten.

safer glass

When a house window breaks, it shatters into sharp pieces that could cut someone.

When a car window breaks, it cracks but does not form sharp pieces.

Ordinary glass is hard but it breaks easily. Broken glass is sharp and can be dangerous. Sometimes glass needs to be stronger to keep people safe.

The glass in car windows is rather like a sandwich. It is made by sticking thin sheets of glass on either side of a thin sheet of clear plastic. If a stone hits a car window, the window cracks, but the glue and plastic stop the glass from breaking into sharp pieces.

Toughened glass is used in the windows of high-speed trains and aircraft. The glass is made in a similar way to that in car windows.

Lenses

Glass can be shaped and polished and made into a **lens**. Some lenses make things look bigger. We often call them **magnifying glasses**. Some other lenses make things look smaller.

The glass in some sunglasses only darkens when the Sun comes out.

The lens in this magnifying glass makes this girl's eye look bigger.

Lenses are found in many things. Spectacles have lenses. So do cameras, telescopes, binoculars and microscopes.

These objects all have lenses in them.

Mirrors

Mirrors are made of glass. A mirror has a glass front with a thin layer of shiny metal behind it. Light bounces off the shiny layer of metal so that you see a clear picture, or **reflection**, of yourself.

The reflection in a mirror is turned round, so that things on the left seem to be on the right.

Some mirrors at funfairs make things look a very strange shape.

Not all mirrors are flat. Some are curved. Curved mirrors make things look bigger or smaller. Many people use mirrors, including dentists, hairdressers and drivers.

This curved mirror at the side of the road helps car drivers to see round a dangerous bend.

Fibreglass

Most glass breaks if you try to bend it. But molten glass can be made into long, thin **fibres** that are bendy. These fibres are thinner than a human hair. When masses of these fibres are put together, they are called **fibreglass**.

Fibreglass being put in the roof of a house. The fibreglass will keep the heat in the house and the cold out.

Sometimes glass fibres are added to plastic. They make a stiff material that is strong and light. It is used to make safety helmets, and the bodies of some cars and boats.

This boat is made from a mixture of glass fibres and plastic.

This hard hat, made of glass fibres and plastic, protects a workman's head.

Recycling glass

The sand and lime used to make glass come from the ground. When they are dug out, big holes are left in the ground. Making glass also uses a lot of heat.

The amount of glass dumped each year weighs the same as 3,500 jumbo jets.

GREEN BOTTLES & JARS ONLY
NO PYREX OR CROCKERY PLEASE

There are bottle banks like this in most towns and cities.

It is possible to make new glass from old glass. This is called **recycling**. Recycling glass means that fewer holes need to be dug in the countryside. It also means that we save electricity and **fuels** such as coal, oil and gas.

These old glass bottles will be taken to a factory where they will be recycled into new glass.

Do it yourself

Make a mirror

1 Find some stiff clear plastic. You could use the clear plastic lid from an old food container.

2 Ask an adult to help you to cut out a square from the plastic.

3 Cut out another square of stiff card, and one of aluminium cooking foil. Make the squares all the same size.

4 Put the foil on the card, shiny side up. Put the plastic on top.

5 Put a thin band of sticky tape around the edges of your mirror. Now try it out. Is it as good as a real mirror?

Glossary

fibre A very thin thread.

fibreglass A substance made from glass fibres.

fuel Anything that is burnt to produce heat or power.

furnace An oven in which great heat can be produced.

glass-blower Someone who shapes molten glass by blowing into it down a tube.

lens A piece of curved glass that can make things look larger or smaller.

liquid Any substance that can flow, like oil or water.

magnifying glass A lens that makes things seem larger.

material Any substance from which things are made.

melt To change something into a liquid by heating it.

mirror A glass or metal surface that reflects something clearly.

molten Something that has turned into a liquid because it has been heated is said to be molten.

mould A container for making things set in a shape that is wanted.

ornament An attractive object or decoration.

recycling To treat waste material so that it can be used again.

reflection The picture in a mirror.

solid Something that keeps its shape; not a liquid or gas.

transparent Clear enough to see through.

Index